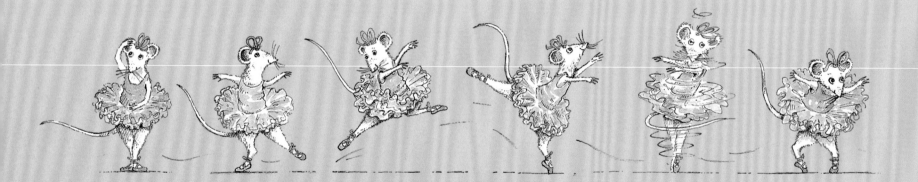

To Tara, Alexandra, and Adam with love —K. H.
To my aunt, Catherine Hope Beddington, with love —H. C.

LITTLE SIMON
An imprint of Simon & Schuster Children's Publishing Division
1230 Avenue of the Americas, New York, New York 10020
First Little Simon hardcover edition August 2019
© 2019 Helen Craig Ltd and Katharine Holabird
The Angelina Ballerina name and character and the dancing Angelina logo are trademarks
of HIT Entertainment Limited, Katharine Holabird, and Helen Craig.
All rights reserved, including the right of reproduction in whole or in part in any form.
LITTLE SIMON is a registered trademark of Simon & Schuster, Inc., and associated colophon
is a trademark of Simon & Schuster, Inc.
For information about special discounts for bulk purchases, please contact Simon & Schuster Special Sales
at 1-866-506-1949 or business@simonandschuster.com.
The Simon & Schuster Speakers Bureau can bring authors to your live event. For more information or to book an event
contact the Simon & Schuster Speakers Bureau at 1-866-248-3049 or visit our website at www.simonspeakers.com.
Manufactured in China 0619 SCP
2 4 6 8 10 9 7 5 3
ISBN 978-1-5344-5151-3
ISBN 978-1-5344-5152-0 (eBook)

Angelina Ballerina

Story by Katharine Holabird   Illustrations by Helen Craig

LITTLE SIMON

New York   London   Toronto   Sydney   New Delhi

More than anything else in the world, Angelina loved to dance. She danced all the time and she danced everywhere, and often she was so busy dancing that she forgot about the other things she was supposed to be doing.

Angelina's mother was always calling to her, "Angelina, it's time to tidy up your room now," or "Please get ready for school now, Angelina." But Angelina never wanted to go to school. She never wanted to do anything but dance.

One night Angelina even danced in her dreams, and
when she woke up in the morning, she knew that
she was going to be a real ballerina some day.

When Mrs. Mouseling called Angelina for breakfast,
Angelina was standing on her bed doing curtsies.

When it was time for school, Angelina was trying on her mother's hats and making sad and funny faces at herself in the mirror. "You're going to be late again, Angelina!" cried Mrs. Mouseling.

But Angelina did
not care. She skipped
over rocks

and practiced high
leaps over the
flower beds until
she landed right in

old Mrs. Hodgepodge's
pansies and got a
terrible scolding.

At playtime she twirled and spun across the playground so fast that none of the little mouselings in her class could catch her, and they were all very cross.

After school she did a beautiful arabesque in the kitchen and knocked over a pitcher of milk and a plate of her mother's best Cheddar cheese pies.

"Oh, Angelina, your dancing is nothing but a nuisance!"
exclaimed her mother.

She sent Angelina straight upstairs to her room and went
to have a talk with Mr. Mouseling. Mrs. Mouseling shook
her head and said, "I just don't know what to do
about Angelina." Mr. Mouseling thought awhile and
then he said, "I think I may have an idea."

That same afternoon Mr. and Mrs. Mouseling
went out together before the shops closed.

The next morning at breakfast Angelina
found a large box with her name on it.

Inside the box was a pink ballet dress and a pair of pink
ballet slippers. Angelina's father smiled at her kindly.
"I think you are ready to take ballet lessons," he said.

Angelina was so excited that she jumped straight up in the
air and landed with one foot in her mother's sewing basket.

The very next day Angelina took her pink slippers and ballet dress and went to her first lesson at Miss Lilly's Ballet School. There were nine other little mouselings in the class and they all practiced curtsies and pliés and ran around the room together just like fairies. Then they skipped and twirled about until it was time to go home.

"Congratulations, Angelina," said Miss Lilly. "You are a good little dancer and if you work hard, you may grow up to be a real ballerina one day."

Angelina ran all the way home to give her mother a big hug.
"I'm the happiest little mouseling in the world today!" she said.

From that day on, Angelina came downstairs when her mother called her, she tidied her room, and she went to school on time.

She helped her mother
make Cheddar cheese pies,

and she even let the other mouselings
catch her on the playground sometimes.

Angelina was so busy dancing at Miss Lilly's that she
didn't need to dance at suppertime or bedtime or on
the way to school any more. She went every day to her
ballet lessons and worked very hard for many years . . .

. . . until at last she became the famous ballerina
Mademoiselle Angelina, and fans came from far
and wide to enjoy her lovely dancing.

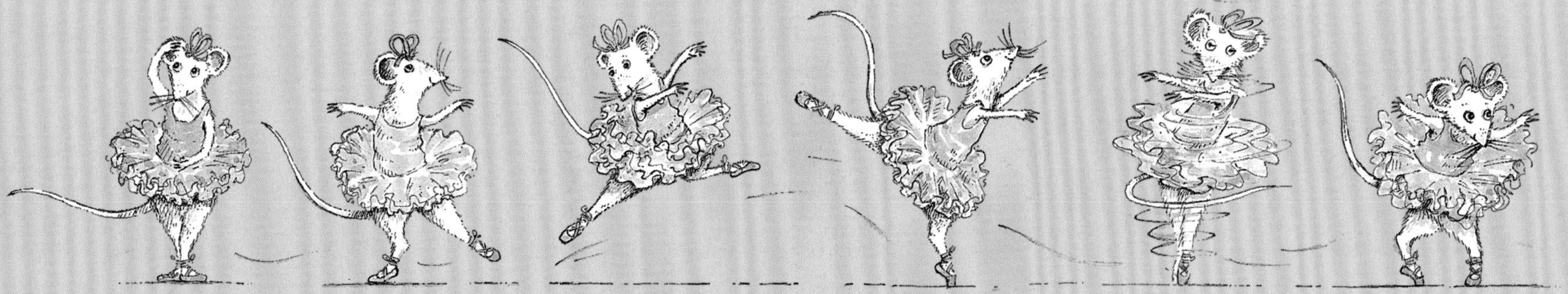